after
SHOCK

" I must have dozed off. Suddenly, I was wide awake. Something was wrong. The rush and hiss of the waves had stopped.

There was silence.

My heart was racing as I sat up. I looked towards the sea and gasped. I jumped to my feet. All I could see was a never-ending stretch of flat sand.

The sea had va~

after SHOCK

after

SHOCK

Jill Atkins

Ransom

SHARP SHADES 2.0

Aftershock

by Jill Atkins

Published by Ransom Publishing Ltd.

Unit 7, Brocklands Farm, West Meon, Hampshire GU32 1JN, UK

www.ransom.co.uk

ISBN   978 178127 982 3

First published in 2016

CONTENTS

ONE

I can't remember how the row started. Me and Mum. We were in the living room of the wooden bungalow.

'And another thing … ' She

pointed at me. 'Your bikini is much too small … '

'Get real, Mother!'

' … And you're wearing too much make-up.'

I clenched my fists.

'My friends wear loads more make-up than me,' I yelled.

'Yes, and just look at them,' Mum ranted on. 'Always in trouble … '

I stomped to the door. Dad looked up from his book.

'I'm going out,' I shouted. 'What a holiday! I thought it would be great, coming to this beautiful place. I'm going to the beach.'

'No!' Mum shouted. She darted after me and gripped my arm. 'You can't. We're going to Babs and Tony's bungalow.'

I shook off her hand. 'Count me out,' I snapped, as I opened the door. 'Does Damian have to go? Oh no! He's scuba-diving.'

'He's older than you.'

'That's no reason. He's always been your favourite … '

'Madeleine!'

That did it! I'm Maddy. She knows I can't stand being called Madeleine.

'I hate you!' I yelled. 'And I know

you hate me. You wouldn't care if
you never saw me again.'

'Maddy … !' I heard Dad call as
I ran out into the sunshine. I took
no notice. He'd make me say sorry.
And *that* I wasn't willing to do!

TWO

I snatched a towel from the rail and ran. I ran past other wooden bungalows, across the grass and under the palm trees. I saw people selling fish and beach mats and

fruit, but I didn't stop until I came to the beach.

The hot, soft sand sifted up between my toes as I walked along. Soon I sat down on my towel. Time to sunbathe. And forget all about Mum.

Slowly, I relaxed. I watched the waves going in and out. I could see three sailing boats out there on the water. A motor boat shot across the bay. People sunbathed. I could hear children's voices as they played in the sand and the sea.

Where was Damian? Out there in the sea. Lucky beggar! I wished I could be scuba-diving with him.

I looked at the palm trees behind me. I could just see the bungalows in the distance.

This was more like it. Paradise!

As I lay down, I felt the warm sand on my back and the hot sun on my face. I closed my eyes. I could hear the rush and hiss of the waves as they moved across the sand. I love that sound.

I must have dozed off. Suddenly, I was wide awake. Something was wrong. The rush and hiss of the waves had stopped.

There was silence.

My heart was racing as I sat up. I looked towards the sea and gasped. I jumped to my feet. All I could see was a never-ending stretch of flat sand.

The sea had vanished!

THREE

It felt like I was in a horror movie.
I screamed. People stared at me, so I
pointed down that long, long beach.
It wasn't like the tide going out. It
was much more scary, as if the sea

had been sucked away. Where had it gone? Seas don't just vanish. Do they?

I screamed again. I could see fish flapping on the wet sand. Adults and children stood where the sea had been. And the boats had gone, too!

I felt sick. I forgot the row with Mum. I just wanted to be with her and Dad. I tried to run, but my legs were limp, like a rag doll's.

At last, I reached the top of the beach, but then I heard a roaring sound behind me. I turned round and froze. There was a giant wall of

water out to sea. And it was coming
my way, fast.

The roar grew louder. The wall
was moving in. I ran, panic rising
inside me. I suddenly knew what it
was – we'd had a lesson at school –
the sucking back of the sea, the
giant wall of water.

It was a tsunami! A giant wave
that rushes in from the sea,
destroying everything. And it was
coming for me. To destroy me!

'Mum!' I screamed. 'Dad! The
sea! It's coming. Get out of its way.'

I saw our bungalow ahead.

'Mum, Dad!' I yelled, as I dashed

up to the door and pushed it open. But they were not there. They must be at Babs and Tony's.

The roar was so loud. The wall of water was still coming. I couldn't take my eyes off it as it came towards me, up the beach and into the trees. I could hear screaming as people saw the terrible danger.

The wave began to lift people and things. It tossed them about like rubbish. It was smashing everything in its path.

I gasped. It was going to lift me and toss me like an old toy.

I didn't want to die.

Did Mum and Dad know a wall of water was going to wash them away? Were they as terrified as me? And Damian! He was in the worst place to be, the sea!

Please, let them be all right.

The roar was louder than thunder. It was getting quite dark. I rushed into the bungalow and slammed the door. Was I safe? I only had seconds to find out.

FOUR

The bungalow shook as the first wave struck. I was thrown against the wall of the bungalow as the wave burst in.

The water was freezing! It took

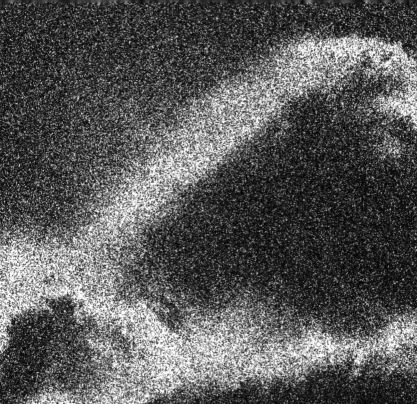

my breath away. I tasted the horrible salty water as it washed up my nose and down my throat.
I kicked my legs madly and pulled with my arms. I was fighting for my life!

I came up for air, coughing and choking. I could see that the water was deep, but the bungalow had not been smashed by the wave.

I swam across the room and grabbed hold of the wooden table. It made me feel just a little bit safer, but my head was almost up to the roof. The water was rising. If it rose any more, I would drown.

Suddenly, there was another loud noise, like an explosion. I hung on to the table as an even stronger wave crashed against the bungalow. Smash! I was washed away. I closed my eyes, held my breath and clung to the table.

The water spun me round and round. I felt dizzy and sick. Soon, the spinning stopped, but I was swept along very fast. The table kept me on top of the water.

I opened my eyes. Ugh! Dead fish, wood, a shoe, a beach mat, a child's toy and a sunshade floated past me. Yuk! I saw a man in red trunks. His

eyes were open, but I knew he was dead. I had never seen a dead body before, except in movies.

Then I saw another body … and another … and another … and another in the water around me.

My arms felt so weak, but I just had to hang on.

FIVE

I'm still alive, I kept thinking. Then,
Mum! Dad! Damian! Where are you?

The wave took me on and on and
on. It was like a long nightmare
where you never woke up. I felt

weak and sick and cold – and very,
very frightened.

But, at last, it slowed down. The
wave crashed onto a rocky hillside.
I let go of my table and hit the
ground hard.

After a while, I made myself sit up.
The water had gone. The land was
beginning to dry in the heat of the
sun. I looked back the way I had
come. I could not believe it.

That beautiful place had been
destroyed. All I could see were piles
of smashed wood, uprooted trees,
upside-down cars, chairs, toys, and

boats sitting a long way from the sea.

But the worst thing was the dead bodies! I would never ever be able to forget that sight. I was shaking all over and fighting back the tears.

I bent over and threw up.

There was a hill behind me.
I decided to go up there, in case the sea came again. And I needed to start searching for my family.

Feeling very wobbly, I stood up. That was when I felt the pain in my left arm. It was hanging by my side. I held it with my right hand as I

began to limp up the hill.

Soon I heard voices... a man yelling names ... a child screaming ... a woman crying. I felt shivers up my spine. I tried to call out, but when I opened my mouth no sound came out.

I looked for my family, but there was no sign of them.

I had almost reached the top of the hill when my legs gave way under me.

Mum, Dad, Damian ... Where are you?

I curled up on the ground and sobbed.

SIX

In the end, my tears stopped. I felt like a zombie. I felt nothing … apart from the pain in my arm.

'Are you all right?'

The voice made me jump. I looked

up at a grey-haired man. He was
muddy and there was blood on his
face.

'Are you all right?' he asked
again.

I shook my head, then stared
towards the sea. It was sparkling. It
made me feel so angry. How could it
look so shiny and calm, after doing
all that damage?

'I'm James,' the man said. 'What's
your name?'

'Madeleine,' I whispered.

That gave me a shock. I went into
flashback. Me and Mum. Madeleine.
My name. That was why I'd said I

hated her and had run to the beach.

'I wish I hadn't said that to her,' I cried. 'Oh Mum!' I screamed. 'Dad! Damian!'

Were they all dead? Thinking of that hit me in the chest like another wall of water.

I jumped up and tried to forget the pain in my arm, as I rushed down the hill. I began searching madly through all the rubbish. I rolled bodies over with my good arm, while the other one throbbed.

There were so many bodies. All dead!

The man had followed me.

'You need to get to a hospital,' he said. 'That arm looks bad.'

I shook my head. 'I have to find my family.'

'My wife, Cathy, and I will take you,' he said.

I frowned at him, wishing he would leave me in peace.

'I can't,' I yelled. 'Don't you understand? I've *got* to find them.'

I moved on, turning bodies over, but praying I wouldn't find them.

'Cathy and I both need patching up,' he went on.

'Go away!' I yelled. But he was still there.

I began to think. *Why was he taking such an interest in me? Where was his wife? Had he made her up to try and take advantage of me?*

SEVEN

The man took a step closer.

'There must have been a big earthquake somewhere across the sea,' he said.

I nodded, remembering that

lesson on tsunamis.

'There's a hospital about a mile … '
James said.

'I said, *No!*'

'We might find your family at the
hospital,' he said. 'They could be
looking for you there.'

A small, white-haired woman
came limping towards us. I could see
blood through the mud on her arms
and legs.

'This is Cathy,' said James.

So he wasn't lying about his wife.

'Hello,' she said. 'Come on, James.
Let's get to that hospital.'

I decided to go with them.

I couldn't carry on with what I was
doing. I was feeling sick again.
I knew I'd have nightmares about
this for the rest of my life.

'Coming, Madeleine?' asked James.

'OK,' I muttered. 'Thanks.'
Before, I might have asked them to
call me Maddy, but now I knew it
didn't matter.

We walked for ages, away from the
sea. It grew hotter and hotter.
I was so thirsty. My legs ached and
the pain in my arm was much worse.
James and Cathy helped me to keep
going.

'We're almost there,' Cathy kept saying.

We met children looking for parents, and parents looking for children. Most of them were crying. We were all heading for the hospital.

At last, I saw a large building ahead, but there were crowds outside. They were all waiting for treatment. And everyone seemed to have come there to find someone.

'Maddy?'

It was Dad!

EIGHT

I burst into tears. Dad hugged me.
I hugged him back, but my left arm
hurt like mad.

'Have you seen your mum?' Dad's
voice was shaking.

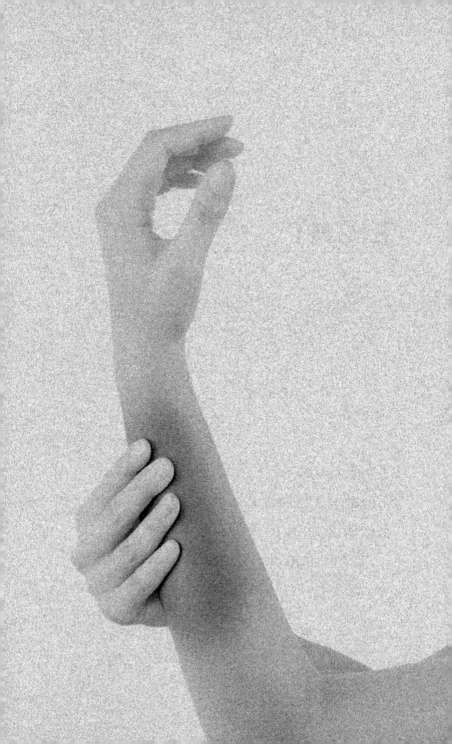

'No.' Then I remembered James and Cathy. I turned to them. 'This is my dad.'

Cathy smiled. 'That's good,' she said. 'Now, you'd better get that arm fixed.'

They went to join a queue.

'Thanks,' Dad called. Then he looked at my arm and frowned. 'This looks bad. What happened to you?'

'I was on the beach,' I sobbed. 'I saw the wave coming … I ran back to warn you … but you weren't there.'

'We were with Babs and Tony,'

said Dad in a dull voice. 'We heard the roar … then, *slam!* It crashed into us.'

'I would have drowned if I hadn't clung onto the table,' I said.

'Tony's dead.'

I felt sick. Tony? Dead?

'I've just seen him … at the back of the hospital. They were bringing more bodies in. And the hospital is full, too. I've been in there looking for you all.'

'Mum? Damian?'

Dad shook his head. His eyes filled with tears. 'Thank God I've found you, Maddy.'

We hunted for Mum and Damian, but in the end we joined a queue to see a doctor.

My arm had to be set. It was killing me! People's faces were pale and their eyes were sad.

It was so hot, but we just had to wait. A helicopter buzzed overhead. Everyone watched it as a large package was dropped out. Someone gave us bottles of water. I guzzled mine down, but it didn't make me feel any better.

Dad left me there while he searched again. When he came back, he

looked ill. He could not find Mum or Damian anywhere.

NINE

At last, a nurse called my name. We went past hundreds of people and into a small room. A man took my photo.

'We'll stick this outside,' he said.

'In case someone is looking for you.'

Then a doctor came in. She looked really tired. I screamed when she touched my arm.

'We'll X-ray this,' she said. 'It's badly broken. You'll need to be asleep when it's set.'

I bit my lip. I just wanted Mum to be there with me.

'You haven't seen my mum, have you?' I asked.

'Sorry.' She shook her head.

I tried not to cry.

'Maybe she's at the other hospital,' said the doctor.

'And my brother, Damian? He

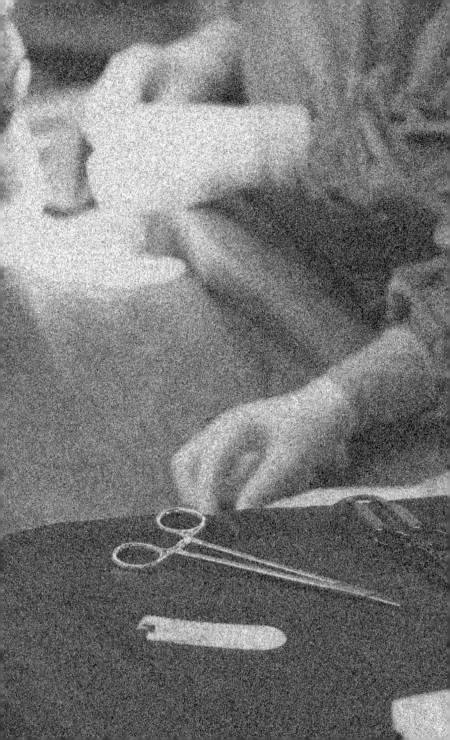

was in the sea when it happened.'

'Sorry,' she said again.

I had to wait for my operation. When my turn came, Dad hugged me.

'I'm going to the other hospital while you're asleep,' he said. He was trying to smile, but his eyes were so sad.

'I wish I hadn't said those things to Mum,' I said. 'I don't hate her.'

'I know,' he said.

When I opened my eyes, Dad was sitting beside me. My arm was in plaster. It still hurt like mad.

'Hi, little sis!'

'Damian?' I whispered.

He was still wearing his wet-suit. It was badly ripped. His face was pale underneath his tan. But he was alive!

TEN

'I can't believe ... how lucky I was,' said Damian, sitting down. 'It was ... terrifying.'

He kept stopping, as if he couldn't breathe. 'Suddenly ... the fish ...

went crazy.' He closed his eyes. 'They knew … it was coming,' he said. 'Then it went dark … and … the sea was … like a washing machine … The water went mad … I clung … to my mate … The sea was trying to … drag us away … '

He swallowed hard. 'There are bodies everywhere … in the sea … on the beach … It's horrible.'

He burst into tears. 'We've got to … find Mum,' he cried.

Dad put his arm round him.

'I found Damian at the other hospital,' he said.

'I got taken there … in a truck,'

said Damian. 'Oh, Maddy … I'm so glad you're OK.'

Dad looked at me. 'How are you feeling, Maddy?'

'A bit sleepy … and my arm hurts.'

'Do you feel OK to leave?'

I sat bolt upright, but I felt so dizzy I had to cling on to Dad for a moment. Then we all stood up. I was so glad to get out of there.

Dad had a soggy photo of Mum. We wrote her name on it and stuck it with the others outside the hospital.

'I bet she's searching for us,' I said.

'She must be worried sick.'

That was how *I* was feeling about *her*! And I wished we hadn't had that row.

As we walked away from the hospital, I kept wishing it was just a nightmare. But I didn't wake up. It was all around us, never going away.

It was growing dark. I wanted to just curl up and sleep, to blot out my worry about Mum.

I love you, Mum, I kept thinking. I hoped that would bring her back to us.

It's the next morning now. Still no Mum.

We didn't search in the dark, but we're setting off again soon.

Did I sleep? I think so. I had bad dreams. Mum was in them all, but I could never reach her.

We're getting food and water and other stuff, and everyone is very kind, but that doesn't really help.

They want to fly us home.

'I'm not leaving without my mum,' I told them.

Dad and Damian feel the same.

We're not going to give up.

We'll find her, even if it takes forever.

The Real Test

by Jill Atkins

Ryan has just passed his driving test. He's desperate to borrow his mum's car and take gorgeous Mollie out for the evening. But Mum keeps saying no. What's her problem?

Flood

by David Orme

It's 2025 and the flood waters are rising in London. Lives are in danger, but Todd's main problem isn't the disaster caused by global warming – it's the drugs gang who are out to kill him.